I0723046

Merry & Bright

Jenn Collignon

Print ISBN: 978-1-7388682-5-4

Ebook ISBN: 978-1-7388682-6-1

For Sofia.

Happy birthday girlie <3

Author's note: When reading this novella, though cozy and sapphic and wonderfully Christmassy, it is important to remember to protect your mental health. There are discussions of loneliness and breakups, swearing, and on-page sexual content between two consenting adults; also, the story hinges on Margot and Jack being stuck in a bookstore overnight with no way to get home, so if that is triggering to you, feel free to pass on this book!

There is one moment of panic, but not related to an anxiety disorder; and Margot specifically is plus-sized and is treated in a very positive light by the text and Jack as well. (We love positive fat rep in romances!)

If any content you come across in this novella is triggering to you, please feel free to put this book down and take care of yourself.

Contents

Audiobooks and Rosy Cheeks

Margot Merry

In Margot Merry's opinion, packing online orders in the back of her bookstore as she listened to a steamy audiobook was the perfect way to kick off her holiday celebrations.

What was being called the storm of the year loomed outside, the wind already kicking up bursts of snow that tinkled against the windows like delicate crystals. She promptly drowned this out by raising the volume on her small Bluetooth speaker.

"Maxwell looked up at her stretched out on the bed, his eyes melting like hot lava as he gazed at her naked body. The Christmas lights around her room glittered in his eyes..."

Books surrounded her in small piles, each crowned with a

crisp packing slip she'd just spent an hour trying to coax her ancient printer into printing. In front of her was the latest purchase from a regular collector who'd been searching for a 1902 edition of Sherlock Holmes' *The Hound of Baskerville* for years. Margot spent twenty minutes earlier wrapping it as carefully as she could in layers of bubble wrap.

It was moments like this, when Margot had the opportunity to source special copies of books for her customers, that made her heart particularly warm. Sure, *Rudy's* was a normal bookstore from the front, selling the latest in any genre, but the back was where the real magic happened. Grandma Rudy had set up a collections room to fuel her love of acquiring antique and special editions of books, and that had spiralled into a lovely little business.

Something tickled the back of her mind, as though someone had called her name from far away.

Margot frowned and hit pause, letting the sounds of the snow and wind outside fill the room again. She hesitated, finger hovering over the play button.

A distant shovel scraped against concrete.

Jack.

Margot abandoned what had been turning out to be an incredible moment of satisfaction for the fictional characters Maxwell and Claire and wove her way around the tiny desk, careful to not dislodge any of the books.

Margot poked her head out the front door, tucking her thick woollen turtleneck closer to her as crisp icy wind cut right down to her bones. "Hello."

The figure shovelling hesitated mid-scrape, frowning. Jacqueline Bright turned, dressed in her usual thick and well-worn sand-coloured winter jacket, her head bare to the elements.

She's missing her usual toque, Margot noticed as she took in Jack's rosy cheeks and red nose. Jack had picked up the habit of shovelling the path up to *Rudy's* for her when it snowed and was often out there throwing down salt to keep the path ice-free. Today, though, Margot hadn't expected to see Jack at all because of the storm coming in.

It was a sweet little Christmas surprise.

Especially since she could picture what Jack's arms looked like beneath her winter coat. Margot had seen Jack knead dough at the bakery enough times during the summer when Jack mostly wore t-shirts that were tight around the arms, so she could —

God, maybe listening to all those steamy audiobooks was getting to her. What was Margot going to do next, start picturing Jack ripping off her turtleneck out here in the cold?

"You know this pathway is incredibly dangerous." Jack's slightly grumpy tone broke through her thoughts. "I've told you again and again, you have to keep this clean."

"Jack."

Jack gestured at the ground around her. "Ice. Winter. Lack of shovelling equals customers who could break an ankle, or worse, their neck." She turned back to her shovel, which was this incredibly large industrial looking thing that she had most definitely lugged all the way down here from her bakery. Margot's tiny little red shovel probably would've barely made a dent in the gathering snow.

"You do know that no one is coming in today. The storm is keeping *most* sane people at home."

Jack stopped again and looked back at Margot as though she was an annoying bit of gum stuck to her shoe. "I'm aware. You don't think that you could also hurt yourself?"

"I'm fairly sure there's no ice, seeing as you shovelled this a few days ago. And de-iced it yesterday morning."

"Packed snow is worse than ice."

"Mhmm, sure," said Margot, frowning at the extra sharpness in Jack's tone. She wasn't the bubbliest of people, but the way Jack was snapping? Something else was going on. "Well, thank you, either way."

Jack simply grunted in response and kept shovelling. Damn, she really had a knack for clearing the snow, and the way that she did a small squat each time made her pants —

Yep, too many sexy audiobooks. Maybe she should divert to a cozy fantasy next.

"Are you closing up soon?"

"I have one more order pick-up in about an hour, then I will be headed home. As should you." Jack sniffed hard and ran the back of her hand across her nose, looking over her shoulder at Margot. "The storm is supposed to hit properly in a couple of hours."

"I've got a few more online orders to sort through," said Margot with a half shrug.

Jack straightened, casting a look around her at the mostly cleared path, which was already starting to build up with a dusting of flurries again. "You should get back inside. You're already turning blue."

"Right. Thanks, again."

Jack traced her eyes over Margot, sending a shiver down Margot's spine. Something about it held a little more weight than the usual look Jack gave her over the counter of the bakery when she went to get her weekly sweet treat.

Those Friday treats had become a bit of a tradition since Margot had received the bookshop from her grandmother. One cinnamon bun, and one of Jack's absolutely divine snickerdoodle cookies. Over that time, Margot had developed quite a crush on the incredibly attractive, tall, muscly baker that spent her mornings kneading dough.

Despite Jack being a bit prickly, there was always a line outside her shop when Margot visited. Margot would tilt her head to the side and catch Jack's eye, the two of them communicating silently across the bakery.

Every time, Jack looked at Margot as though she was trying to read her like a book. Trying to examine every little detail of her face, any flicker of expression.

Without fail, Margot would blush furiously as she waited her turn, every time.

But now?

"Is everything okay?" she asked, hesitating. Jack jumped slightly, as though she'd forgotten Margot was there.

"What? Oh, yeah. Yeah, fine." Jack nodded emphatically, almost too many times, before she scratched the back of her head and turned away, taking her shovel with her. "I'll uh — I'll see you around, Margot."

"Merry Christmas, Jack," said Margot softly as Jack walked down the lane. Margot shivered from the cold and turned to head inside, glancing once more after Jack's strong silhouette heading back toward the bakery before heading back to her stack of orders and her audiobook.

"Claire held onto Maxwell's hand as though it was a lifeline as she gazed off toward the towering office building, wondering what

would be held inside those shining dark windows. What kind of possibilities, what kind of a future they held. Once, she would've been scared. But with Maxwell at her side, anything felt possible."

Margot sighed happily as the audiobook came to a close, her pile of online orders long since finished, stacked up and waiting for when customers would come and pick them up. She'd been sitting there alone, listening to the story as it came to its climax, watching the growing storm through the back window.

Without the audiobook running, the rising wind outside was much louder as she stepped into the main shop. It was rather eerie to hear as icy snowflakes tap danced across the windows, alerting the true start of the storm. She gazed around the space once more, picking up her empty to-go mug that had held a cinnamon latte hours ago, and dropping it into her tote bag.

Drip.

Margot froze, eyes darting around the main shop, catching on the old battery-powered Christmas lights she'd strung up along some of the shelves, the aged silvery tinsel tree absolutely smothered in ornaments her grandmother had collected from bookstores around the country, and the darkening sky outside.

Drop.

Her head whipped toward the collections room door that was slightly ajar. She'd checked in on those books earlier, running her finger along the delicate spines and covers, smiling at them all tucked comfortably in their shelves.

Drip.

Margot sped inside, dropping her bag next to the entrance with a clunk and threw the door open, flicked on the light, and witnessed pure horror.

Drop.

"No!" she gasped out, frozen as she looked up to the large, swelling bubble on the ceiling that dripped every few seconds – right on top of a shelf that held some of the antique books. Margot's eyes widened as she watched the puddle of water on top of the shelf splash with yet another *drip* from the ceiling.

"Oh, no no no no –"

The bubble loomed dangerously as Margot lurched into movement, gathering up as many books as she could.

2

Nostalgia and Fruit Cake

Jack Bright

"Oh, Jack, thank goodness you're still open. It's an apocalypse out there!"

Jack blinked up at the man who'd just walked into her bakery, pausing mid swipe as she scrubbed the bakery front counter for the fifth time that afternoon. Her thoughts had wandered to the beautiful bookstore owner, curves on full display in that absolutely perfect turtleneck that made Jack want to run her hands all over Margot Merry.

At least she hadn't been thinking about the fact she should've been on a plane by now. Or that she would have to be spending Christmas alone instead of by a roaring fire, her family by her side.

Just like that, the sour mood she had been battling all day settled back around her shoulders.

She eyed the windows beyond the man's shoulders, noticing that the snow had started to pick up. But still, it was barely anything close to a blizzard. *Apocalypse.* This poor man had no idea what was coming.

"I'm open just for you, Miguel. How's the weather?"

"Absolutely terrible," Miguel shivered, his entire body trembling under the fridge-like winter jacket he regularly wore during the winter season. He looked like a bright red marshmallow on steroids. "I don't know why you didn't go somewhere hot this Christmas. For me, at least. You should have gone *for me.* I couldn't because my wife's whole family would roast me over the fire if I mentioned going home, so no no, fair or not, I am here with your Canadian winters freezing to death, going out and picking up my beloved mother-in-law's favourite Christmas cake before she decides that she wants to break my nuts in that awful nut-breaker, or whatever you call it."

Jack couldn't help but chuckle. Despite her crankiness at having to cancel her flight to the prairies for Christmas,, she couldn't help but smile.

"Well, we best get you home quickly then, before the apocalypse turns into a blackhole, or turns you into giant nutcracker."

Miguel made a sound like an angry goose in the back of his throat and put up both hands. "Knowing my mother-in-law..." he shook his head and chuckled along with her. "Go enjoy your Christmas, Jack."

Fat chance of that happening, thought Jack as she forced a smile onto her face for Miguel, sliding the two tightly packaged Christmas cakes across the counter. The cakes had finished baking a few hours before but the rich scent of browned butter underlaid with the sweet, fragrant bite of cloves and various dried fruits that clung to the air. Despite herself, Jack breathed in long and slow, drawing that perfect scent of Christmas in, mingling with the freshly zested orange and the sweetness of candied peels that rested on the cakes.

She should be smelling this perfectly nostalgic scent from an expensive candle burning in her sister-in-law's kitchen as a turkey roasted in the oven, all the while holding a newborn baby and keeping her eldest niece Bree, who was four, occupied to give her parents a break.

"Get home safe," Jack said to Miguel, passing him an extra bag of pastries she'd packaged, hoping to pawn off as many as she could so that she wouldn't have to lug an egregious amount home in the storm. There was no telling how long she would have to wait out the storm once it hit; leaving baked goods to go stale hurt her soul. "Give those to your kids, tell them they're from Santa. Or, you know, tell them they're *for* Santa, and leave them out with milk for you to have a midnight snack."

Miguel guffawed and tucked all the goodies inside of his marshmallow jacket. "Have a wonderful Christmas. Feel every bit of the magic with your heart."

"Careful on the sidewalk, I de-iced it this morning but there's a nasty patch that likes to fight back."

Miguel waved in thanks and ducked out into the cold.

As the door closed, Jack let out a long sigh. Despite the smell of Christmas lingering around her, there was nothing festive or magical happening in her heart. For weeks, she had been planning on closing up her bakery early and hopping on a plane to go spend Christmas with her family; but of course, the "storm of the year" had appeared on radars and every plane headed out of their tiny little town and neighbouring city was grounded, taking her perfect family-filled holiday right out of her hands.

Carmen and Avery had just had their second child, which was like a special kick to the gut by the universe. Jack *loved* babies, especially those that her sister-in-law and brother made. Plus, having one at Christmas like some little perfect miracle wrapped up in a little red and green onesie? It was cruel of the universe to rip away her Christmas cheer like that.

Now she would have to figure out when she would be able to take another break from the bakery to go visit them in the new year; but by then, that newborn scrunch was going to be all gone, and the Christmas magic long lost to the new year's drag.

At least she had Loaf. Jack shook her head and wiped her hands on her pants, moving to the back where she had piled her things, ready to go. Loaf, or as her brother had named him Sir

Bread Loaf of the Crumb, was her beloved staffy; a tail-wagging tank the size of a suitcase and the weight of a table, waiting ever so patiently for her at home.

Jack chanced one more glance out the front window as she slid on her jacket, eyeing the flurries with suspicion. At the moment, they weren't getting too bad; but, knowing her luck, by the time she got home, she would have to convince Loaf to even think about stepping out into the snow and cold to go for a walk he very much needed.

Cinnamon and the smell of sweet, soft butter wafted up from the bundle of pastries she'd thrown into a large brown paper bag before she grabbed the knobbly, overly bright rainbow toque that Carmen and Bree had knit for her last Christmas and pulled it on. She'd worn it today specifically, hoping that the reminder of her niece's brilliant smile as Jack had unwrapped the hat and immediately put it on her head would lift her spirits.

It, at least, kept her ears warm.

"Alright Pete, let's go."

She retrieved a mason jar almost the size of a newborn baby from beneath the counter. Inside, her sourdough starter wiggled happily, knowing very well that the reason she even had to bring the godforsaken thing home in the first place was that, if left unattended for more than two days, Pete the sourdough starter was going to have an explosive reaction to being left alone.

That reaction might cause him to break through his *fifth* jar, despite having more than enough room within.

That's why she had given the starter a name. Because there is nothing anyone could say to convince her that that bubbling mass of dough was not *sentient,* let alone alive as it fermented and summoned bacteria to make absolutely sublime bread. A sentient being that often needed attention was nothing if not a man.

So "Pete" it was.

Jack shouldered her way through the front door after she'd turned all the lights off and checked every single heat-inducing appliance for a sixth time to ensure they were switched off. She tilted her head up briefly, frowning at the gloomy, churning grey sky as snow descended around her, getting caught by gusts of wind every few beats, swirling up and around, dancing their way to the ground.

Thinking only of Loaf and a large bowl of leftover macaroni and cheese, she set off down the dark street, the Christmas lights draped about the lane swaying in the growing wind. Their town had strung the soft, glowing white strands around the streetlights and across the lane itself, creating a rather picturesque holiday scene when filled with shoppers. It was almost romantic, walking beneath it, with the snow whirling around her.

Many of the shop owners had packed up the day before,

deciding to simply stay home today, in case the storm arrived early.

I wonder how Margot fared today, Jack thought in passing, her head turning automatically to catch sight of the bookshop down the lane from hers. However, unlike the other dark storefronts, the lights still shone in *Rudy's*, Margot's old-fashioned Christmas lights glinting colourfully around the window frame.

Margot had been so excited about finding those pink and teal lights online. They were classic Christmas light colours that no longer existed and were battery powered, so they were entirely safe to use. She had actually brought them down the lane to show Jack when they had arrived, her face lighting up. Jack hadn't had the heart to tell her that she had zero idea of their history, let alone that pink had been a Christmas light colour.

Though, Jack would give it to the bookseller on one thing: those lights immediately brought out a deep, nostalgic feeling of an old Christmas movie.

Jack walked up the path that she had shovelled just a couple hours before, her boots making perfect prints in the skiff of snow that had already laid itself down atop the concrete. She knocked and peered inside, squinting to see if Margot was visible. There was movement near the back of the shop, but after a beat of no one answering, Jack twisted the door handle and opened the door to chaos.

3

Harry and Marv

Margot Merry

Margot's thoughts were locked on one thing and one thing only: save every single book from risk of ruin by water.

"Margot? Are you still here?"

The voice jarred Margot so hard she nearly dropped the stack of antique books she had in hand.

"Jack." Margot peeked between the stacks and noticed the woman standing in the entrance to her bookstore. What was she doing here? "Just one second. I — I, oh *fuck*, that's — AGH!"

"Hey." Jack rustled behind her as Margot turned back to the room with the threatening water bubble that was growing by the second. A moment later, there was a strong arm sliding around Margot's shoulders, carefully stopping her and turning her around. "What's going on?"

Margot stared, slightly crazed, into Jack's face. She blinked a couple times, registering Jack's brilliantly lumpy rainbow toque and the pink tint to her nose. Jack took the stack of books from her and set them carefully down on a nearby shelf.

"Margot?" Jack's hands squeezed her shoulders before her rich brown eyes narrowed and came closer into view as Jack inspected her. "Are you okay?"

"Sorry. Yes. No — *No.*"

"No, you're not?"

"No." The word came out like a half-sob, pitching up in octave. "Jack, the books. *The books.*"

Jack looked around her, wary, as though she was expecting some horrifying creature to pop out at them. "What about them?" Then, after a slight pause, "Where did all these old books come from?"

"The collections room," Margot choked. "Jack, there's a leak upstairs. It's —" she let out a soft wail as a solid *drip drip drop* noise sounded.

"There's a leak from the café?"

She peeled away from Jack without answering and immediately launched back into cleaning mode, gathering up as many books as she could in her arms.

Jack stepped into the room after her, halting in her tracks. "I didn't know this room was here."

"It's only for collectors," Margot wheezed under the weight

of about fifteen hefty tomes. The corners of some of the books were digging into her soft belly and arms, but she didn't care. She just had to get these books *out.* "Grandma Rudy set it up decades ago, you know how she was."

Jack instinctively reached out and grabbed the new stack from Margot, blinking in wonder around at the room. Then her eyes landed on the slowly growing bubble.

"Shit."

Margot let out a high-pitched laugh and started to gather more books haphazardly.

Jack frowned at the bubble, as though it had appeared just to spite her. "I'll help."

Margot opened her mouth to protest, half realizing that Jack was still in her winter jacket and hat, before the woman set down the towering stack of antique books carefully on the floor next to her and peeled off both. Her short hair puffed out in a halo of static that Jack didn't seem to notice before she bent back down and scooped up the books almost effortlessly.

"You don't have to," Margot finally said, watching irritation cloud Jack's expression. Jack obviously did not want to be there, didn't want Margot's problem getting in the way of her evening and getting home safe before the storm started. "I can figure this out myself."

"Two sets of arms are better than one."

"Alright." Margot blinked, trying to ignore the little voice in the back of her mind that said *especially your arms,* her attention snagging on the way Jack's overshirt clung to her muscles and back as she left the collections room.

"Where do these go?"

"Just—" Margot cleared her throat and followed her out with her own stack of books, gesturing with her chin toward the middle of the room. "Anywhere on top of shelves or a chair, keeping them off the floor in case we get flooded."

Jack turned to Margot with a slightly exasperated look. "Okay. First up, that's not going to happen. If it is a leak from upstairs, you would need enough water to fill a swimming pool to even begin to flood the place, which would cause damage not just to the books but to the walls and floor and everything else. And that's not going to happen," she added as horror spread through Margot's gut, "because we're going to get all the books out of that room and then deal with the leak."

About ten minutes later, they had managed to pull all of the shelving and books out of harm's way of the bubble that now was continuously dripping water. Jack vanished into the back room, hunting for a bucket, as Margot tried to calm her heartbeat.

If she'd lost those books, she had no idea what she was going to tell her grandma. Grandma Rudy had been the pioneer of this shop and the collections room in the back. That room and those books had been the hardest for her to give up when she retired and handed the keys to Margot; it was like a second grandchild to her.

A good chunk of those books were from her grandma's own collection, not for sale and only for Margot to take care of, including a practically priceless copy of Jane Austen's *Emma*. The book was part of a third edition Clarendon Austen set, which contained Austen's six published novels, and ran upwards of five thousand dollars when all together, but Grandma Rudy would never part with it for any price. The memories wrapped up inside those pages between Margot and her grandma made the book priceless.

Margot wouldn't part with it either.

She clutched the copy of *Emma* to her chest and breathed. Jack reappeared with a bucket and step ladder, which she placed right below the bubble.

"We're going to have to pop it."

"*What?*"

"Carefully," said Jack, looking up at it. "I don't want it bursting and getting everywhere. If I can pop it directly into the bucket, at least we don't have to worry about getting more water everywhere. I know you're not technically supposed to, but the chances of us getting someone out here to properly pop it before the storm hits are slim to none."

Jack patted down her jeans before she grabbed her winter jacket, withdrawing a pocketknife from inside. Margot raised the bucket for Jack, trying to not panic at the idea of popping a giant water bubble above her shop.

"You may want to step back," said Jack, taking a step up.

Margot nodded and retreated, watching as Jack reached up with both knife and bucket, trying to find a spot to provoke the deluge of water to release. She managed to poke a hole in the side of the bubble, wiggling her knife around until a solid stream of water started to pour out.

Margot quickly rushed off to find a broom, then reached up to help guide the water out of the hole, squeezing it out like a tube of toothpaste, easing the pressure on the bubble. After a matter of minutes, they were able to leave the bucket on the ground beneath a slowly dripping leak, the ceiling bubble nothing more than a large mark of wrinkled, saggy paint.

"Now that that's taken care of." Jack glanced her way before walking over, rubbing her hands together. "Have you tried the Owenses?"

"The café owners?" Jack shot her a look. "Right, obviously. No, I haven't. Why would I be calling them?"

"The leak is coming from their café."

Margot gave herself a mental shake for being so short sighted. She was going to have to tell them about the leak, and potential damage. "Right."

"We're going to have to stop the leak before any more damage happens. We can't just leave it as is."

"How on earth are we going to do that?" Margot squeaked, watching as Jack turned and started walking off toward the side door of the bookshop, the secondary, indoor entrance to the café upstairs.

"Do you have a key?"

Margot shook her head. "They never gave me one."

"Do you know where they may keep a spare?"

"Nope."

"Great." Jack beaconed for Margot to follow. "In that case, we are going to break into the café."

Margot pulled out her phone and hit dial to the family that owned the café upstairs, first for Mark Owens, then his wife Clara, and as a last resort their son, Liam, all of whom had been on vacation down south for a couple of weeks.

Every call ended with their voicemail box.

"Well, no one can say we didn't try to get a hold of them." She bit her lip and looked at Jack uneasily, who was currently examining the locked door to the café. The stairwell that ran along the side of her bookstore was almost as cold as if it had been outside, despite the outside wall encasing the space. It was lit by a single overhead bulb at the top, casting everything in a chalky white light. Margot hated that overhead light with all her being, but nothing she said could convince Mark Owens to replace it, as it was some kind of special sunlight bulb he had spent *so much* time finding, and spent *so much* money to get.

It was really a crime against her eyes.

"So, we're really going to do this?"

"Yep."

"Just... breaking in. Committing a crime, two days before Christmas."

"We're the veritable Harry and Marv. Just have to make sure Kevin isn't around to catch us."

"Where did that come from?" Margot's face split into a smile and she laughed, the sound filling up the stairwell around them.

Jack looked over her shoulder at Margot, a soft gleam in her eyes, which completely took Margot by surprise. "What? It's not like I don't know *Home Alone*, one of the greatest Christmas movies of all time."

Margot shook her head as Jack turned back to the door, crouching down in front of the handle. "Do you know how to pick a lock?"

Jack snorted. "People don't know how to do that outside of books and movies."

"You were crouching like you were about to try."

"I was crouching to inspect it," said Jack, immediately straightening. She rubbed the back of her neck and gestured at the door. "Best chance we have is either Google, or simply kicking it down."

"The less damage, the better."

Jack pulled out her phone and started to type into Google as Margot shifted back and forth on her feet, trying to not pick at the skin around her fingernails. Instead, she considered Jack; from her still slightly staticky hair and the frown that creased her forehead to her broad shoulders, down to the hips and thick thighs that had, on occasion, made Margot think incredibly dirty thoughts.

Like right now, since Jack was squatting in front of the door, her jeans strained in a rather spectacular fashion.

Just as Margot was beginning to sink into one of those dirty thoughts that involved something very close to what her audiobook had been narrating earlier, Jack stood, took a step back, and kicked in the door.

4

Cinnamon and Break-Ins

Jack was rather proud of herself that kicking the door had even worked. She cringed slightly at the loud *SLAM* as it crashed back against the wall, but besides that, the door was open much faster than if she had spent however long pretending she knew how to pick locks.

Margot squeaked in surprise. "Jack!"

"Well, it worked."

Margot's cheeks were flushed when Jack glanced back at her. Margot tucked a bundle of her glossy dark curls behind her ear in the way she did when she ordered at the bakery, pretending to look up at the board as though she didn't know exactly what she was going to order every time. Jack bit the inside of her cheek to hide her smile.

Jack cleared her throat and gestured. "After you."

Jack stepped back to let Margot pass into the dark interior of the cafe, watching the way a small little crease appeared between Margot's eyebrows.

God, Margot was so pretty when she worried. Whenever that little crease appeared, it made Jack want to kiss it smooth.

Not the time, Bright, she chastised herself internally, following Margot inside. *You have a leak to worry about.*

Jack inspected the damage that her kick had done. The strike plate had flown off, peeling some of the wood with it; the door frame was cracked, and the interior trim had snapped off with the impact of Jack's foot.

"Shit," she breathed, running her thumb along a bit of it. 'Least damage possible,' wasn't that what Margot had said? Yeah, right.

"Right. Now we just have to..." Margot gestured into the cafe vaguely. "Find the leak. And somehow stop it."

Jack turned around in the dark space and oriented herself, trying to picture the layout of the bookstore below them. Amidst the shadows of tables and chairs that had been flipped up out of the way when the Owenses had closed for the holiday, there was only light coming from the two large corner windows directly across from where Jack and Margot stood. A tree outside swayed and bucked with the rising storm winds.

Jack assumed that the leak would've been from the café bar,

where the Owenses had recently installed a cleaning system for washing mugs and glasses, but Margot's collections room was further back than that in the building. She headed toward the back, where the two bathrooms were. "I think your collections room is… Yeah, should be right back here."

Jack nudged the door open and flicked on the switch inside, letting out a low whistle. The toilet was running continuously, a thin layer of water pooling on the floor as it overflowed.

"Shit," she repeated her expletive from before.

"Do you know anything about plumbing?" Margot hovered tentatively by the door.

"Enough to know how to turn off the water, which should be at least a temporary fix to this situation and stop it dripping into your bookstore." Jack crouched down and inspected the back of the toilet, locating the knob to turn off the water that ran directly to the toilet. Immediately the hissing stopped. "The Owenses can deal with the actual leak-fixing when they get home."

"I'll go see if I can find towels and whatever to try and clean this up."

Just to be safe, as Margot was off investigating the rest of the cafe for cleaning supplies, Jack dipped under the sink and turned off that tap too, and the ones in the next bathroom which was dry.

The last thing that Margot needed was for her entire bookstore to be flooded if the rest of the plumbing decided it was going to cause issues.

"I think we're going to use up their stock of towels," Margot's voice drifted over before she did as Jack stood and turned off the second bathroom's light. Jack stepped back into the partially flooded one as Margot handed her a roll. "Paper and other wise. There's not much left in their storage room. Here."

Their fingers brushed momentarily, electricity sparking between them. Jack sucked in a soft breath as Margot's bright eyes found hers, flicking up in surprise.

"It is really quite dry in here," Margot said, a tiny smile breaking across her face, as though she was trying to hold it back. "Your hair is, uh."

Jack grimaced and ran her hand over her head, trying to coax her hair back into some semblance of a hairstyle, and not a ball of static and frizz.

"Well, since that's fixed, you can go." Margot nodded to Jack and gave her a grateful nod. "I'm sorry to have interrupted your evening."

"It was no problem." Jack flicked off the bathroom light behind them as they made their way back to the door.

"I appreciate the help."

The two of them stared at one another for a few heartbeats in the middle of the cafe. In the silence that rang out, all the buzzing humming ring of electricity coming to a halt, the howling of the wind outside sent shivers up Jack's spine. It had gotten quite dark out in the moments that they had been up here, sending the cafe into shadows of shapes, barely visible.

BRRRING, BRRRING, BRRRING -

Jack's heart practically leapt out of her chest as Margot let out a soft gasp, her ringtone loud in the empty cafe.

"Hello? Oh, hi Mark, thank goodness you got my message... no, no, there wasn't much... well, Jack and I got the books out of the way before it could get really bad, but... yes, we're up here now..." Margot turned a little aside as she talked to the cafe owner.

Jack stuck her hands in her pockets and waited, half-listening as she watched Margot out of the corner of her eye.

For the longest time, Jack had tried to stop herself from developing any kind of feelings for those she worked around, especially those she saw on the regular like Margot. It was a little rule she had instigated a number of years back after she dated a clerk from the little gift boutique down the way, because that had gone *very* badly when everything fell apart.

But there was only so much one could do when faced with such a beautiful, kind woman who had incredible tits and a tummy that Jack wanted nothing more than to run her hands all over.

Plus, the woman had such a penchant for cinnamon and butter that she practically kept Jack in business. Not just in the colder seasons either, when it made more sense to bake with those seasonal spices. Margot Merry's cinnamon addiction spread through all the seasons. Jack had taken to making special batches of pumpkin snickerdoodle cookies just for her.

Jack wasn't a huge reader, so she didn't have a regular excuse to go to the bookstore until she started to bring Margot her cookies. Plus, it was a rather happy coincidence that the café above *Rudy's* was Jack's absolute favourite spot in town. Their coffee was absolutely sublime, and she got to see Margot, even if just in passing, daily.

Though, at this point, Jack would do anything to see her smile. Like shovelling the bookstore's sidewalk.

Right now was not the time to realize exactly how deep of a crush she had on this woman, Jack thought, running her hand through her hair.

"... great, thanks. I'll make sure to lock up all the doors downstairs when I leave, just to be extra safe. Have a great rest of your vacation, and happy holidays, Mark."

Margot hung up the phone behind Jack with a soft sigh. "Jack, you don't need to stick around any longer. I've got it from here."

"I..." Jack blinked at her, frowning. "I want to be here."

"Do you? Really? You don't seem like it."

Jack deflated slightly and chuckled, rubbing her face. She supposed she had been kind of short and snappish all evening. "I'm sorry, I'm not very good company today. I... I was supposed to be on a plane today to visit family, but the damn storm came in and crushed those plans."

"Oh," Margot said softly, nodding. "I completely forgot that you were supposed to be visiting them for Christmas. I'm so sorry. I know the storm has caused a lot of folks' holiday plans to be upended. Didn't your brother and his wife just have their baby?"

"They did," said Jack, a soft, true smile breaking across her face. "They named her Noelle, fittingly."

"Oh, that's lovely." Margot placed a hand on Jack's arm. Jack marvelled at it, trying to hold herself together. She couldn't remember the last time she'd been touched so kindly by someone else.

Jack sighed before trying to wave away the heavy feeling settling back into her chest, only now realizing that it had basically vanished when she was helping Margot. "When I can sneak away, I'll book another flight after the holidays are over to go and meet her. Give Carmen a week off of parent duty, let her sleep and take care of Bree for them. But I should... I should be there, you know? I should be there to help. Noelle is so new, and I know how hard it was for Carmen with Bree, and I wish... I just wish I could be there."

Margot's eyebrows contracted in sympathy. "Oh, Jack, I'm so sorry. What a shitty time for a storm to hit, hey?"

"Not your apology to make, unless you can control the

weather." Jack half smiled at her.

Margot opened her mouth to say something else, but right then, there was a distant BANG and the light in the stairwell went out. The streetlights outside flickered and died, throwing them into much darker shadow and silence, except for the howling wind outside.

"Shit," hissed Margot.

"Storm must be getting bad," said Jack, moving toward the window. That turned out to be an understatement.

In what felt like mere moments since Jack had walked into *Rudy's*, the entire world outside looked as though the entire North Pole's worth of snow had been dumped from the sky. Wind buffeted snow this way and that, swirling in a torrent of flurries so thick that Jack couldn't see the stores across the way.

All that was left was a blanket of white, swirling snow.

Jack whistled long and low, shaking her head.

"Oh. My. God," breathed Margot from behind Jack as she carefully made her way over to the window. "How are we going to get home in this?"

"I don't think we are."

"Hey, Susan, it's Jack," murmured Jack into her phone as they both stood in the middle of Margot's bookstore in near complete darkness. The only light source now was Margot's battery powered Christmas lights, which illuminated the edges of the windows that looked out onto the hellscape that was the winter storm outside. Even the usual white nighttime light that reflected off the snow was grey and clouded by the storm.

Susan, Jack's neighbour, answered with a cheery, slightly concerned voice. "*Jack! Are you alright? Where are you? Are you still at work?*"

"Yeah, I got stuck at work later than I wanted waiting for a customer, then I stopped by to help Margot with some trouble at the bookstore."

"*Oh, gosh, is she okay? Did something happen to her in the storm?*"

"No no, she's totally okay, there was a small leak." Jack glanced up between her eyelashes at the dark store around them. Margot had vanished into the backroom, her phone flashlight searching.

"*A leak! How terrible, right before the holidays.*"

"Yeah, terrible, but no books were harmed, thankfully." Jack cleared her throat before continuing. "Susan, do you mind checking in on Loaf for me? I don't know when I'll be able to get home, and I don't want him to panic with the storm —"

"*Oh of course. The girls and I will head over right now and bring him here, so he isn't all alone in the dark. How does that sound, girls? Go get your coats — we're going to go rescue Loaf!*" Susan spoke away from the phone before the sounds of excited cheering started up on the other end.

"Can we also make snowmen?" called a distant voice on Susan's end of the phone.

"Sure, why not. It'll be buried before morning, but what can I say," Susan said quieter into the phone.

"Thank you, I appreciate that so much. Tell the girls I will bake them each a cake for taking care of him. And you, whatever you like."

"You can make it up to me by coming to my New Year's Eve party this year, since you're home for the holidays. Bring me that fabulous rhubarb and cranberry cake you made that one time."

"Ah, yes, sure. I'll do that."

"And you can bring your — well, I don't know *if you're seeing anyone,"* Susan's voice sounded upturned with hope, as though Jack was going to spill some secret love that she had kept hiding. As though she could keep anything hidden from her nosey next-door neighbour. *"But if you are —"*

"No, I'm not seeing anyone, so I'll take a rain check on that."

"Are you sure?"

Jack sighed and shrugged to the darkness around her. "I'll bring Loaf."

"Oh, the girls would love that. Okay, we're off, boots are on and coats zipped. Loaf, here we come!"

"Thank you again, Susan."

"Of course, any time."

Right. Well, at least Loaf wouldn't be alone tonight — and, she supposed, she had New Year's plans that would prove to be interesting, if not eons more entertaining than staring at her walls wishing she was holding a newborn baby.

Jack straightened slightly then, frowning. If she was going to be here with Margot all night, she didn't want to bring the evening down with her mood. Plus, it sounded like something straight out of a rom com to be stuck in a bookstore overnight with a beautiful woman.

She sucked in a long breath before letting it out, long and slow, forcing the thoughts of her lost Christmas plans out of her mind. She could go back to sulking about it tomorrow, if she could make her way home. Right now?

Right now, she was going to spend her Christmas Eve eve with Margot Merry.

5

Magic and Music

Margot Merry

Margot rooted around in a storage bin until she located an industrial flashlight and clicked it on, setting it down on a table to help illuminate the space as she continued to poke around.

She was trying to pretend that she hadn't eavesdropped on Jack's phone conversation, but it was hard, seeing as everything else in the bookstore was dead quiet.

No girlfriend?

She wasn't entirely surprised, seeing as Jack had never spoken of a significant other practically ever since Margot had known her. She knew that Jack dated, of course, and there were rumours that curled around their little street a few years back concerning her and one of the previous clerks of the nearby shops, but nothing recently.

Margot always wondered what it would be like to spend the holiday season with a significant other. Whenever the holiday season came around, Margot found herself single and curling up with her books. Even back when she was a teenager, she preferred to be mostly alone, aside from her grandmother. But now Grandma Rudy had retired down south, so it was just Margot. She tried not to think about how much lonelier it made her feel around this time of year.

She imagined it was quite lovely, to be with someone you loved so much. Romantic and soft, with the Christmas lights on, the old Christmas songs on the radio softly crooning in the background.

"Need any help?"

Margot jumped as Jack's voice came from right next to her, jolting her from her thoughts. "I was going to try and clean up the store a bit before heading home, so that no mildew would get into the books, but now with the blackout and the storm, I don't think I can get any fans running, and the towels I can find might not be enough."

Jack cast a quick glance around the shadowed back room. "We can at least get those fans set up in case the power comes on while the towels soak up whatever they can."

"Here," said Margot, finding another flashlight and handing

it to Jack before she started to unearth the fans one by one.

The two of them set to work, angling the few fans the store had around the collections room, before laying out whatever towels they had grabbed from the café above and weighing them down with a storage bin and the step ladder. Margot left the plugs sitting next to the wall for whenever the power came back on, all lined up neatly on the floor.

"Don't you want to try and get home?" said Margot, curling her arms around herself.

Jack opened the front door of bookstore and was immediately buffeted back by a gust of snow and icy wind, the front mat immediately dusting over white as snow fell inside. There was already a mound building up along the front of the shop, the pathway that Jack had shovelled earlier for her completely filled in. The street beyond was nearly invisible as the snow worked to erase the features outside.

"I don't think I'm going anywhere, either."

Margot breathed in long and slow, eyeing Jack. "So it's a night in the bookstore, with no heat." All night. Together.

"I'm sure your grandma has blankets stored somewhere in here." Jack tapped the cover of a book nearby. "While we're here, we may as well organize a bit of the chaos that the leak caused. So you don't have to after the holidays."

Margot nodded slowly. "It's something. But we don't have any food, I don't keep any in the shop."

"Good thing I've got all my things with me," said Jack. She smiled as she lifted a brown bag in the air, the sight easing some of the nerves racing around Margot's chest. "We've got dinner covered, as long as you don't mind having strictly bread and pastries."

"That sounds like a perfect feast."

Margot grabbed her speaker from the back room and started up some Christmas music. The shop was too empty without it as she and Jack settled into the evening.

Soon, soothing tones of Frank Sinatra covered the storm that raged outside.

A bit later, after Jack had served them both muffins to tie them over for a little while longer — making sure that Margot got the cinnamon apple one — they started to poke around the store together. Margot used her phone flashlight to scan the covers and spines of the books, slowly starting to put them in some semblance of order atop the lower shelves in the middle of the shop.

Jack started to flip through a few, carefully opening the covers, and inspecting the titles. "Your grandma started this whole collector thing? Is she into it, or did she do it just for the store?"

"She collected books herself and knew of a couple folks in town who did — soon, they started using the backroom and then it spiralled into a business." Margot tapped the cover of a particularly lovely copy of Shakespeare's poetry that was leather-wrought and in the right light still had gold leaf in spots on the cover. "She fell in love with it, hunting first over the phone, in person, and then online when she got the shop connected to the internet back in the late eighties. She found every bit of the collection specifically because it would be a hit with those who regularly sourced books through her, or it was a piece she particularly wanted to add to her collection. It's her pride and joy."

"Yours as well."

"What?"

Jack leaned against the shelf nearby. "I see the way you look at these books and talk about them. Sure, you love the bookstore itself, but I think you have a bit of your grandma in you when it comes to these collectors items."

Margot couldn't help but smile. "You think?"

"Absolutely. Though, I do question why someone in the store picked up a stack of magazines from the seventies about aliens. That one is a weird choice."

Margot burst out laughing as Jack held up a magazine that had a slightly blurry image of a stereotypical green alien on the front with the headline **ALIENS: THE TRUTH YOU NEED**

TO KNOW. "That's from a previous employee. Sometimes the employees would be allowed to buy a few things for the shop, to see if they would sell, and this one guy, Bruce, had a passion for aliens."

"Didn't he know that aliens only work for the public in content that usually is classified science *fiction*? Not these weird magazines that supposedly reported — oh look at that, a UFO sighting in the middle of the Duck Mountains. Who knew we had sightings up here in Canada, too."

"I think he bought them through the shop so that he could have a reason to read them himself," said Margot. "Grandma usually stopped his alien purchases, but sometimes they slipped through. I wonder how many of them still exist in the shop."

The two of them started to root through the shelves, trying to find the alien books that were left behind by the infamous Bruce. They got sidetracked and turned around a few times, finding funny joke books and random pamphlets people had shoved in the romance books section about *seeking God*.

Eventually, they headed into the back, hunting for blankets. A chill had begun to settle around Margot from the lack of heat in the shop. Thankfully, Grandma Rudy had kept a veritable treasure trove in the back. They found blankets, candles, a couple stools that would work great as little individual tables, and an old stash of Christmas themed mugs.

She shifted a particularly thick quilt out of a box, revealing a small camp stove. "Hey, look at this."

Jack shifted closer with her flashlight and angled it into the storage bin. "What on earth did Grandma Rudy need that for?"

"Who knows," said Margot, chuckling. Beneath, there was a little sauce pot, the perfect match to the stove. "But I think if we want, we could make some hot chocolate. I think the Owenses won't mind if we take some of their special syrups either, seeing as we stopped their café from flooding."

A cozy, cave-like atmosphere fell over the shop as they brought together a few bits, beneath one of the largest windows lit with battery powered Christmas lights. Margot brought over a few of the other strands, detaching them from other windows to drape on the shelves around them, trying to brighten the space.

She'd co-opted a couple of the squishy armchairs from around the store and tucked them in against the window at an angle. Then, she draped a couple blankets over both, before squishing another one on the floor, mashing and fluffing until it all looked rather purposefully cozy.

Candles were dotted around the bookstore, each on a plate to protect the shelves and books from errant wax and flame.

Jack returned from the café upstairs, arms full of as many syrups and bits she could hold, dangling two mugs at the edge of her fingers. She winked at Margot and set up a little station atop the front desk, clearing out a space so as to ensure that no liquid got onto any of Margot's papers.

"Fire up that little stove, Merry. We've got hot chocolate on order."

"Alright, Bright," said Margot, shooting Jack a smile as the woman set herself up behind the desk like a proper barista, pouring some milk into a small saucepan to set it to boil, before dumping in a few packets of powdered hot chocolate.

"What will it be? Cinnamon? With a few marshmallows and a pump of vanilla to sweeten it up?"

Margot scoffed playfully. "How did you know?"

"You don't think I notice your cinnamon addiction? I figured you would take it in your hot drinks, too."

"And the marshmallows and vanilla?"

"Extra sweetness. I know you, Margot."

Margot felt a sweet, soft warmth spread through her chest that had nothing to do with the prospect of hot chocolate and marshmallows. She pulled out a couple marshmallows and stacked them in a misshapen snowman on the counter. "And you, I know, will take yours with caramel drizzle and as many marshmallows as you can fit in your mug."

Jack eyed her, something gentle shining in her soft brown gaze.

"I know you, Jack," said Margot, repeating what Jack had just said to her. "And, it helps that the café you usually get coffee from is right above me."

"I've never had hot chocolate from them, though."

"Coffee sweetened to a level of a tooth ache with lots of milk — and I know you love the added whip. I always see you licking it off your finger as you come down the stairs."

"Maybe I should retire from barista-ing," said Jack with a soft chuckle, lifting a mug. If Margot wasn't wrong, Jack was blushing, but it was hard to see by the light of the tiny little stove. "You seem to know your way around these things."

A slightly fake chocolatey smell purveyed the shop as the hot chocolate heated through, Jack mixing the sauce pot with a tiny whisk to incorporate all the powder into the boiling milk. It reminded Margot exactly of cold winter days when she came inside after tobogganing or making snowmen with friends, finding her grandma with a mug of hot chocolate waiting for her, piled high with marshmallows.

Jack poured their mugs, adding in the accoutrements, before they made their way over to the cozy corner.

As she sipped her hot chocolate carefully, testing how hot it was, she watched the raging storm. Jack reached forward and pulled her blanket down over her shoulders for her, brushing her fingertips against Margot's shoulders. Despite wearing a turtleneck, Margot's skin erupted in goosebumps.

Margot's voice caught in the back of her throat, unable to form words. It was such a simple, kind gesture, but as they sat here in their own little world, it felt entirely perfect.

Something had changed over the last few hours as they settled into the darkness of the store — as though the two of them were the only two beings alive right then, in their little snow globe world, as the storm raged outside of the soft glowing Christmas lights reflecting on the windows.

She could practically feel Jack's eyes on her, which made her sip her hot chocolate too soon, burning her tongue.

"What's with the old Christmas music?"

Margot chuckled to cover a cough. "Grandma used to always play this kind of Christmas music around the holidays in the shop, so it just feels right. There's good Christmas music coming out now — but I will say, there is nothing more Christmassy than the originals."

The softly crooning voice of Billie Holiday swirled around them, punctuating her point as the atmosphere turned distinctly more Christmassy. It helped, too, that the air smelled syrupy sweet with the vanilla, cinnamon, and the hot chocolate.

"The new music today, I think, is too commercialized."

"I would believe you if I hadn't caught you singing along to Mariah Carey the other day," said Margot playfully.

"It's too catchy! It gets carved into your skull, the amount of times they play it on the radio. I think they even started playing it early November this year, which is criminally early."

"I like it," said Margot loftily. "It makes everything from the incoming stretch of bleak November weather to the flurries and the icy mornings coming into work more bearable. Then of course, when you actually hit December and it's more socially acceptable to have the music blasting and the decorations pulled out from storage, it just adds a layer of spice to the air."

"That elusive Christmas spirit," sighed Jack.

"Elusive?"

Jack waved a hand half-heartedly. "You know."

"You mean in the way that it never feels the same from when you were a kid?" Margot scanned her face, watching the way her mouth turned down. "Or just this year?"

Jack gazed down into her hot chocolate for a moment, as though inspecting the way the one lone marshmallow that hadn't yet dissolved floated around the lip. "There's always that lingering loss, when you grow up and stop believing in that magic. But you always seem to have a great mood around Christmas, with your endless cinnamon-filled treats and your kitschy Christmas décor."

"I'd go with timeless, but okay."

Jack snorted. She pointedly glanced toward one of Margot's many Santa figurines nearby that was wearing a suit jacket made entirely of pink tinsel. "Sure, we'll go with *timeless*."

"I don't think anyone ever escapes that loss of magic," said Margot. "It comes with growing up. Becoming an adult, paying bills, having to get a *job*. But there's something that I think all of us still chase around the holidays, that feeling we used to feel, making it in any way we can. I do that in throwing Christmas into every inch of the shop, making sure that the atmosphere is perfect."

"And I usually do that by spending Christmas with my family, especially my niece." Jack shook her head slowly. "At least I know that as soon as Bree gets a look at the presents under the tree, she'll completely forget I even exist," said Jack with a soft, self-deprecating laugh. "But it's for me, really."

"What is?"

"Spending Christmas with my family. Watching Bree go through the things I did as a kid, waking up with those lovely glowing lights, the morning cast in such anticipatory joy with the family around — even with the fights that could come about because someone accidentally gave Grandpa too much eggnog the night before, or what have you — it's all Christmas to me."

Margot smiled, putting herself back into her childhood memories of waking up to find her grandma waiting at the foot of her bed, a Santa hat perched jauntily on her head, with a grin so bright it instantly made her happy. 'Santa came for you,' she would say, even as Margot grew up and learned the truth about the figurehead, determined to keep some kind of magic alive for Margot.

"It's like watching those old black and white Christmas movies that were always more sad than happy — those hold a perfect flavour for being an adult at Christmas," said Margot, her voice soft and quiet in the bookshop. "They lack that classic joy of building a snowman and bringing it to life with magic."

"Frosty really did know how to do it — he just ran from his problems."

Margot snorted into her hot chocolate. "Maybe that's what we should do. Make ourselves into snowmen and go run off and find Santa."

"It's a deal, Merry. As long as you don't melt on the way. I could never handle that." Jack clinked her mug against Margot's with a soft, eye-crinkling smile that made Margot's insides burn. "I just realized, I never asked. Do you have any Christmas plans?"

"I have a ticket booked for the second week of January to go visit Grandma Rudy — sometime after the Christmas rush, when the planes are a little quieter," answered Margot. "She's probably down there having the time of her life. But for the meantime I had plans to settle in with a good book, maybe a couple of Christmas movies. It's my favourite time of year to just bury myself in comfort."

"You don't get... lonely?" Jack looked up at her through her eyelashes. "I shouldn't pry, but you're not seeing anyone... are you?"

"I'm not," said Margot with a soft laugh. "It can get lonely, of course, but I've kind of made my peace with the quieter holidays. Though I would love, one day, to have a full loud boisterous kind of Christmas. Family, love, laughter. All that. I know this isn't really the kind of Christmas you were wanting, and is probably a whole lot less noisy than you wanted, but... I'm kind of glad you're here with me, at least. It does make the solitude a little more bearable."

Jack's cheeks flushed and she laid a hand on Margot's knee, running her thumb over the fabric of the blanket covering her. "I do actually like being here with you, Margot. Quite a lot."

Their little bubble of light suddenly felt too tight and close. The heat of Jack's hand seemed to sear directly into Margot's skin, despite the layers of cloth that separated them.

If she wanted, she could move just an inch, and they would be touching, she could practically lean over and kiss Jack if she wanted to —

Margot blushed before she stood abruptly, tossing the blanket off her shoulders, on the edge of doing something foolish like *kissing her friend in the middle of a blackout* and started off toward an opposite window that looked down the street.

6

Fuses and Flashlights

"The streetlights are on again," said Margot, running out of their cozy corner so quickly that for a handful of heartbeats Jack couldn't quite process what had happened. Margot had been so close to her, and the way that she had looked at Jack was almost... *hungry*.

Did Margot... like her? Did Margot *want* her?

The thought sent Jack to her feet, following Margot to the window where the storm raged outside. She had to know, had to get close again, to see if it was just her imagination. All this time, she'd been operating under the assumption that Margot hadn't felt any kind of way toward her but friendship — there hadn't been any signs that Jack had noticed over the years of them knowing one another.

Their reflections shone back at them like ghosts against the darkness, but there was one solitary yellow seed of light in the middle of it all from a streetlight further down the lane.

"Huh, look at that. That's odd, isn't it? In a blackout?"

Margot watched her through their reflections, her lips open ever so slightly, that damn crease back between her eyebrows. She rather looked as though she had just been lost in a book and interrupted.

Jack glanced down at the small space between them, Margot in her soft knit turtleneck that hugged her curves, and Jack's hands just inches away.

Just try it. See what happens.

The inches vanished as Jack placed her hand on Margot's waist, sliding in behind her a little closer. Margot's body heat radiated through the soft fabric so intensely that Jack's breath caught in her throat. She had to hold herself back from drawing all of Margot to her, enveloping the woman in her arms and never letting go. She was so *warm,* and she smelled like cinnamon and chocolate. It was all together too intoxicating.

Margot started to lean back, but then, as though shot through with electricity, she shot away from Jack and started walking quickly across the store.

Jack blinked after her, suppressing a shiver at Margot's absence. "Where are you going?"

"The basement," she said. "What if it's a fuse that's tripped and we've just been sitting here in darkness?"

Margot's face shone in the harsh white glow of the flashlight as she popped open the electrical box, her face furrowed in concentration.

Jack, of course, was thinking only of the moment that Margot had leaned back into her at the window. She sighed and blinked down at her own hand, which was buzzing slightly as though it could still feel the texture of Margot's sweater.

Get a grip, Bright.

They were currently in the basement of the bookshop, surrounded by incredibly dusty, musty air, and a layer of grime on the floor that probably hadn't been shifted since Grandma Rudy had run the shop. If Jack thought about the dust too much, she would probably start sneezing.

It was also so cold that their breath was starting to become visible around them.

"Do you know anything about fuses?"

Margot frowned as she looked at the positively insane array of fuse switches in front of her, controlling not only the bookshop but the cafe above them as well. "Not a damn thing, other than sometimes, if I use my air fryer, stove top, and my microwave all at the same time at home, something will suddenly stop working and I just have to go —" she mimed flicking one of the fuses back on, "and everything is good."

"That's basically all the knowledge I've got, too," said Jack, remembering when her dad had dragged her into the basement after her old gaming system had blown a fuse. He was adamant about showing Jack the proper way of doing things, but she'd been fourteen at the time, and only wanted to keep playing, not listen to her old man tell her the reason fuses did what they did. She scanned the box above Margot's head, her sight only slightly blocked by Margot's brilliant dark curls, which — *god, Jack, why are you like this?* — she was momentarily distracted by as the thought of running her hands up through them, pulling them slightly taught, as she kissed Margot senseless.

She cleared her throat and forced herself to blink a few times before she properly scanned the fuses. None of them appeared to have been tripped at all.

"Mm, no, it looks like it's a proper blackout. Nothing's wrong."

Margot let out a soft noise of annoyance. "Then why are the streetlights on outside?"

Jack quickly pulled up her phone and typed in 'streetlights on in blackout.' "Apparently, some streetlights can be powered by a different part of the grid, compared to businesses and the like."

"Huh."

"You learn something new every day."

Margot turned around and looked up at Jack, her lashes fluttering as she must have realized, right when Jack did, that they were incredibly close together. The expression on Margot's face stilled, the frown lessening to something almost blank, as her eyes focused on Jack.

"Sorry about the blackout," said Jack, her voice low, almost a whisper. Margot's face melted into something warm, her eyes charged with... something that Jack couldn't put a name to.

"It's not your apology to make," she said, her voice equally as quiet as she repeated what Jack had told her earlier. "Unless you control the grid."

The laugh that escaped Jack was nothing more than a soft chuckle.

"I'm sorry that you have to spend your Christmas Eve eve with me," Margot whispered. "If I could, I'd take my weather powers and simply will the storm to calm enough for you to fly off to Christmas with your new baby niece."

Jack laughed. "I don't think I would change anything about today, actually. Being here with you has made what would have just been me sulking in my apartment with Loaf stewing in sadness something much more... sweet and I have to thank you for that."

Her hand reached up and tucked a curl behind Margot's ear on its own accord. Margot sucked in a tiny breath, so minuscule that if Jack hadn't been nearly pressed up against her in this dark basement she wouldn't have noticed. In the single beam from the flashlight, Jack watched the tiniest crease appear in Margot's brow before her eyes flicked down to Jack's lips.

"N-no problem," answered Margot breathlessly, before she dragged her gaze back up to meet Jack's.

Jack's heart skipped a beat.

Were they about to kiss in the kind of dingy, overly dusty basement beneath Margot's bookstore? That was not what Jack had planned in her head for their first kiss, let alone any kiss, though there were probably some stranger, more passion-filled thoughts hidden deep in the back of Jack's brain where they were doing many more things than just kissing in the dust-filled basement.

Probably. Most definitely. One hundred percent, her brain was cooking them up ferociously, as though she was writing her very own fan fiction for the two of them.

BRING! BRING!

The two of them launched apart as though shocked by the non-existent electricity as Jack's phone started to ring, cutting the sound between them.

She breathed almost raggedly into the phone. "Hello?"

"Hiya Jack! How're things?"

"Hi, Susan," said Jack to the voice coming through her phone, Susan her neighbour's cheery tone masked slightly by bright conversation in the background. She shut her eyes and shook her head at Margot with a small smile on her face. "Things are okay, here. Still in blackout, though, and I'm fairly sure we're fully snowed in for the night."

"*Oh, the girls are going to be so happy about being able to wake up with Loaf here. Though, I will probably have to break up a fight between them as to who gets to have him sleep at the end of their bed.*"

"He'll love it, I know he will."

"*I just wanted to check in, because we're listening to the radio and apparently the power is out across town,*" said Susan. "*Roads are closed, they're not even going to have the ploughs out until morning, if you can believe it. And, I also wanted to let you know that Loaf is doing great. We're all here huddled around a bunch of candles, under blankets, and — get this — the girls have built a fort under a bunch of them with Loaf inside! I think they're telling him stories.*"

Jack smiled and chuckled low under her breath, picturing it in her mind. "I'm so glad."

It took a few more minutes of talking to get Susan off the phone, but once she did, Jack let out a long, low breath of air, feeling jittery and as though her skin was being kissed by thousand tiny lightning bolts.

"Shall we go back upstairs?"

Margot, who had been busying herself with her phone, it seemed, looked up at Jack and nodded. "Since the fuses were kind of a bust."

Jack ran her hand through her hair, shivering involuntarily. An absolutely insane, totally bizarre idea crossed her mind.

When in a blizzard...

Margot grabbed the flashlight from Jack, momentarily casting her face in shadow. Without realizing what she was doing, Jack followed the movement, closing the gap between them until she could practically feel the body heat emanating from Margot.

Instead of reaching down and kissing her senseless, which was all that Jack could think about, she said, "Let's go make a snowman."

7

Snowmen and Parkas

Margot Bright

"A snowman?"

"A man made out of snow. Or a woman. Or someone non-binary, of course. A being of snow, if you will." Jack mimed the shape of a snowman in the air. "I think it could be fun."

"But it's cold out."

"That's what winter is, Merry. Didn't you bring a jacket?"

Margot rolled her eyes and laughed. "Yes, of course I did."

"Good."

When they arrived back up in the bookstore, Jack pulled on her winter jacket as she peered down at a large mason jar that Margot recognized as her sourdough starter.

"Pete staging a coup?"

"Not yet," said Jack, patting the lid with affection. "Alright, Merry. Get your coat. Let's go see what this blizzard has to offer."

The smile that stretched across Jack's face as she placed the third ball of snow, making the head of the snowman, was enough to melt Margot's heart. Something about it, the shine of her eyes beneath her bright rainbow toque as her cheeks turned red from the cold, the snow swirling around them in the momentary lull of the storm, felt as though she was standing in the middle of a snow globe. Everything was lit in a hazy, dull glow of the single streetlight and the Christmas lights that lined the bookshop windows.

"Too bad we don't have a carrot nose," said Margot, running her mittened hands over the surface of the snowman to smooth it out.

Jack took off one of her mitts and reached out with a finger, poking two holes for eyes, then seven more for a mouth. "We shall just have to use our imaginations. But I think ol' Frosty here won't mind."

"It's a pleasure to meet you, Frosty," said Margot, miming a handshake with the snowman as Jack shuffled around it, carving out a better space within the drift for them to stand in. "I am happy to have you as guardian of my bookstore."

"Why thank you for having me," voiced Jack from somewhere behind the snowman, putting on a fake deep voice. "I rather like the thought of books. But I think I like baked goods much more."

"Do you now?"

"Things so thick with cinnamon you cannot taste the sugar beneath!"

Margot scoffed at Jack as she poked her head around Frosty's body, scooping up snow as she did. "Oh yeah?"

"Ah!" Jack ducked as Margot threw the snow at her, half formed into a hasty snowball.

"Come back here!"

"You just wait —"

The two of them launched into an impromptu snowball fight, using Frosty as cover. Margot succeeded in planting a snowball directly into Jack's toque, almost knocking it free.

"Hey, no head shots!" shouted Jack. "Didn't you ever learn the rules as a kid?"

"No, which makes sense, because I don't follow anyone's silly rules. That hat is so bright it's practically a painted targ — JACK!" Margot shrieked as Jack came running at her, holding onto the back of her jacket and dumping snow inside.

"That's for almost making me lose my prized toque."

Margot laughed, the sound swirling up with the snow around them, her cheeks so cold that she couldn't quite feel them anymore. She picked up a handful of snow and threw it at Jack, not really caring if it formed a ball or anything other than a cloud in the air, the two of them breathless with laughter. She chased after Jack, throwing handfuls of snow at her.

At the last second, Jack spun around. Margot squeaked and sped off past Frosty, toward the front door, laughing as Jack chased her.

"No!" Jack roared happily, ploughing through the snow just an arm's length away. "You're not getting — AH!"

Jack's lower body shot out from beneath her and she ploughed into Margot, the two of them collapsing in a large snowbank together. Muscly, strong arms fastened themselves around Margot's waist, holding her close, as the two of them stared at one another, panting, both smiling as though they were kids again.

There was a beat, just between breaths, where Margot's world sharpened to just Jack. Right here, with her in the snow, surrounded by the storm with their cheeks reddened and eyelashes coated in snowflakes —

Kiss her.

The thought was a bolt of electricity down Margot's spine. Should she?

She glanced down at Jack's lips, the smile and half open

mouth as she laughed, and thought, fucking hell, if this isn't it, then when? What was she waiting for?

But before Margot could move, Jack closed the distance and kissed her, stealing her breath away.

She tastes like chocolate and snow and her nose is freezing, thought Margot before her mind narrowed in on nothing but the fact that she was *kissing Jacqueline Bright* in the snow.

Margot tried to extricate her arms from between her and Jack so that she could wrap them around Jack's neck, but when she found she couldn't, instead she settled for curling in closer. Jack made a soft sound in the back of her throat, something between a gasp and a moan and deepened the kiss. Between heartbeats, the world around them was nothing more than frosted breaths and the sound of the storm.

Jack peeled back from her suddenly with a sharp gasp, blinking wide eyes, as though she had just been caught stealing a Christmas present from a child. "Shit, I'm so sorry. I shouldn't —I—"

Margot started laughing, which was obviously not the right reaction, because Jack looked even more terrified.

"I shouldn't just be *kissing you* out in the snow like that, I should've asked, I, shit I'm —"

"Don't you dare say you're sorry again," interrupted Margot. Then, because she could, she leaned forward and kissed the *sorries* right out of Jack Bright.

They broke a part a moment later, Margot slightly breathless. "You're kind of making my Christmas, Jacqueline Bright. Do you know how long I've had a crush on you?"

"I'm... I'm making *your* Christmas?" Jack's expression melted into soft, giddy happiness and she laughed. "With you right here, saying that, kissing me the way you did — you made not only my Christmas but my whole damn year, Merry. God, why didn't I ever just get over myself and ask you out?"

"You wanted to ask me out?"

"Every time you came into the bakery, asking for your damned cinnamon treats."

Margot laughed as Jack leaned in, pressing their foreheads together.

"This could technically be considered our first date, then," said Margot. "Even though we stumbled into it a little backwards."

"What, you've never accidentally fallen into the girl you like and kissed her in a snowbank before?"

"No, I can't say that I have," she teased.

"Well." Jack kissed Margot on her nose. "I highly suggest it sometime. And don't worry, I'll take you on a proper first date once this storm is over."

Margot finally managed to extricate her arms from between them and wrapped them around Jack's neck. "Good." Then, "I think my pants are soaked through."

"Mine too. But I don't particularly care."

"Oh?"

Jack simply smiled and kissed her again, pulling her closer still. Margot crinkled her nose as Jack placed a cold mitten on her cheek, laughing through their kiss, before Jack's urgency dragged her back down.

A moment later — or perhaps it was minutes, hours, days, Margot couldn't say — they separated, Margot leaning her forehead against Jack's lips.

Margot started to laugh. "Oh my god, wait, you actually *fell*. Are you okay?"

"I think so?" Jack laughed, reaching up and adjusting Margot's hat with a cold, snowy mitten. "I told you you should've shovelled this damn sidewalk."

Margot opened her mouth, playfully affronted, and shoved Jack's shoulder. "You'll have to take that up with my personal shovel girl. She comes every morning there's been snow, without fail, to shovel the pathway for me."

"Oh yeah? What's she like? Some super sexy type, who shovels in her bikini or something?"

"I wish," snorted Margot. "If you ever did that, I'm getting the evidence tattooed on my body. Right across my forehead, so I can see it every time I looked in a mirror."

Jack laughed before kissing Margot again, the ferocity of which sent fire right down into Margot's core. When they broke apart, they were both breathless anew, and Margot wondered how unsafe it would be to unzip Jack's parka and hers in the middle of a blizzard, because she was becoming positively overheated with the need to feel Jack's skin on hers.

"Jack?" she murmured between kisses.

"Mm?"

"Can you walk?"

"Maybe. Why?"

"I want to go back inside." She looked at Jack up through her lashes, her heartbeat racing, before she kissed Jack again.

"You want to stop?" Jack breathed.

"I want to go — somewhere warmer — so I can take — your clothes off," answered Margot, drawing Jack up with her.

"Hmm," Jack hummed in the back of her throat, before she broke their kiss, playing with Margot as she held her lips just a breath away, a teasing smile breaking across her lips. "Are you saying you don't want to get naked and risk frostbite for me?"

"Jaqueline Bright, right now, I'd risk anything," Margot gasped as Jack started to kiss along her jawline and down her neck. She leaned back, her eyes half open in pleasure, the flurries above them swirling in the fog of her breath. Margot clutched at Jack's parka as she began to unzip Margot's, her mouth travelling down the length of her neck.

"I love your sweaters usually but right now, it's kind of in the way."

"Jack," Margot gasped. "*Please*."

Jack scooped Margot in a rustling of parkas brushing together, wrapping both of Margot's legs around her hips. "All you had to do was ask nicely."

Margot cackled as Jack brought her back inside, over to their little corner of light, kicking off her winter boots as she walked. With a quick swipe, Margot removed both her and Jack's hats, kissing her all the while as Jack put her down once more.

Immediately, Margot threw her boots off, followed quickly by her jacket. She started to shimmy out of her ice-cold jeans that were soaked through. Jack paused, her eyes shining in the glow of the Christmas lights, watching her struggle.

"You need help with those?"

"Maybe," said Margot, making a face at the sensation of the fabric clinging to her.

"Just ask."

"Please help me, Jack," she breathed as Jack dropped to her knees, still half in her parka, in front of Margot. Her fingers hooked into the hem of Margot's jeans and slowly began to work them down Margot's thighs. Jack's eyes flickered in the candlelight as she gazed at Margot, before she leaned forward and started a trail of kisses down the front of both her thighs, following the descent of her pants.

"Margot fucking Merry," Jack breathed her name as Margot stepped from her jeans and kicked them away. Jack was looking at her body with such reverence that Margot shivered involuntarily. "You are so beautiful, you know that?"

She reached out to cup Jack's cheek, wanting to see her beautiful face but instead, she got pinned by the burning need in Jack's eyes.

Jack kissed the inside of Margot's hand before leaning forward, Margot's fingers travelling through her short-cropped hair. Jack's mouth trailed kisses along the tops of Margot's legs as her hands caressed the back of Margot's calves, sending a current to the Margot's core.

"Jack," she breathed, her need almost bringing her to her knees. "Please."

"Please, what?" Jack murmured, dragging a finger along the back of one of her thighs.

"I... I need..."

"Tell me what you need, baby," said Jack, as that finger started to play with the fabric of Margot's underwear, teasing along the soft skin. Margot's legs widened on their own accord, allowing Jack to see more of her, wanting Jack to see everything.

"Take them off," she said, barely audible.

"As you wish, Merry."

In one swift movement, her underwear was off. Both of Jack's hands travelled up the length of Margot's thighs and to her ass, holding her steady as Margot leaned into a nearby shelf.

"*Fuck*, Margot."

Margot didn't have a moment to answer — didn't even care that there was a particularly sharp book digging into her skin right then — because Jack chose that moment to bury her face between Margot's thighs.

With one caress of Jack's tongue, Margot could have melted the snow outside with the heat that ran through her. She gasped, clutching at Jack's hair, holding her closer.

"You taste so good," Jack hummed, adjusting herself so one arm held onto Margot, steadying her, and also spreading her a little wider. With a searching finger, she parted Margot's folds gently, running a fingertip along the slickness gathered there. "How's that?"

"S-s-so good," stammered Margot.

"Like this?" Jack slid a finger in, before following it with a second. She then did something with them that sent a whole new set of shivers up Margot's spine. "Or this?"

"Ah — ah — oh god, y-yes — there —"

Jack chuckled against Margot's skin and started to slide her fingers in and out faster, working her tongue and lips over Margot's clit as though she knew exactly where Margot's pleasure was centred. After a moment she slipped a third finger in, causing Margot to grip Jack's hair so hard her fingers started to dig into the woman's scalp.

"*Jack*," she moaned, the sound drawn out as she started to crest faster than she thought she could. "Oh, oh I'm —"

"Come for me, baby," panted Jack in between her incredible ministrations with her tongue, her voice gravelly with desire. "Come for me, just like that."

As though the words were a spell, Margot came apart, her moans turning into an incoherent mess of noise as her knees gave way. Jack held her up against the shelf with one hand, following Margot to her climax with practiced movements with the other.

Slowly, achingly, Margot blinked back to some form of consciousness, clutching Jack's head to her stomach, her body being held up by Jack's incredibly strong arms.

"Jack," she breathed, unable to say anything else.

"Good?"

"Fuck yes," Margot said, pulling Jack up from her knees so she could kiss her. "You, Jack Bright, are wearing too many clothes."

8

Holiday or Sinatra

Jack Bright

Jack couldn't think straight as she looked at the beautiful woman standing before her, half naked, coming down from her orgasm.

Fuck, she was so sexy.

Margot started to clumsily pull at Jack's clothes, yanking her parka off of her shoulders, followed by her overshirt and t-shirt. The moment Margot's hands came into contact with her bare skin, Jack thought she was going to explode with the need pouring through her. She was desperate to see and feel every inch of this woman.

She started to try and pull Margot's sweater off — why the *fuck* was she still wearing it, Jack would never know — but Margot pushed her back, fighting for the waist band of Jack's snow-soaked jeans.

"These first," she said.

"You," said Jack, her voice a rasp of want, "are so fucking sexy."

Margot looked up at her through her lashes as she fought with Jack's belt. "I am?"

"God, yes."

It took only a moment later for her to step out of her jeans and to pull Margot over to their corner of coziness all the while kissing the woman everywhere she could reach.

"This," said Margot, running her hands along Jack's chest, currently bound by the rather ugly sports bra she had thrown on this morning.

"What about it?"

"Off."

Jack didn't need much more telling than that. Off it came, the cool air inside the bookshop instantly sending goosebumps across her now exposed skin. Margot's hands hovering over Jack's skin as though she was worried to touch her.

Jack reached over and dragged Margot's sweater off of her, throwing the damned piece of clothing away, before feasting her eyes on Margot. God, she was *so beautiful.* Every curve, every soft turn of her tummy, the delicious swell of her chest, made Jack's entire body ache. There was just one more thing that needed to be removed. "You too."

Margot smiled rather coyly as she slid a hand behind her, unhooking her own bra. "What, is Jack Bright a tits girl?"

"Tits, ass, tummy," answered Jack as Margot teased her, holding onto the front of her bra, slowly revealing her *incredible* tits. "All of it. All of you."

She kissed Margot all over, wanting to explore the woman's entire body, all of the curves and softness of her, with just her mouth and hands. They leaned back into the blankets, Jack's hands cupping and holding as much of Margot as she could. There was *so much of her* to love. She wished she had ten hands to be able to worship the woman the way she deserved to be.

Margot ran her nails down Jack's back, arcing up in pleasure as Jack pulled one of Margot's nipples into her mouth. Then, the woman's hand travelled down, lower, achingly so, until she slipped her fingers beneath the waistband of Jack's underwear.

Jack hummed her pleasure as Margot started to wiggle, trying to reach lower. The sensation was already almost too much for Jack, want and pleasure warring with each other to keep kissing this beautiful woman or let the woman have her way with her.

"Jack, let me —"

"Just a minute," said Jack, kissing along Margot's one breast before going to the next. "These ladies need to be properly greeted."

"*Jack.*"

Margot trapped her lips in a kiss filled with fire, both of Margot's hands searching across Jack's body. She let out a soft gasp right into Margot's mouth as the woman somehow managed to grasp both her ass cheeks with strength she had no idea the little bookstore clerk could have.

An almost feral laugh escaped Margot's throat as she squeezed, flipping Jack just enough so she could squirm down lower, sending little bolts of electricity across Jack's skin as Margot sucked and kissed her across her collar bone.

Margot slid one hand along Jack's thigh, drawing her leg up over Margot's own, before she locked eyes with Jack.

"Merry," said Jack, unable to say anything else. She couldn't help moving her hips, wanting friction, wanting touch, *anything* to relieve the want between her legs.

Tingling fire alit along Jack's stomach and ass as Margot's nails started to playfully drag along her skin.

She should be considered the eighth wonder of the world, Jack thought, in a complete daze of pleasure as Margot smiled wickedly before kissing her again, their tongues dancing and teasing.

Jack couldn't help the soft moan that shuddered through her as Margot's fingers finally found their goal. She slipped them in between Jack's legs, touching, testing, before she found her clit.

"In or out?"

"J-just l-like that," stammered Jack.

"Good girl," purred Margot, clutching Jack closer as her hand worked pure magic. Jack bucked and humped against her, unable to control herself.

"Call me that again," she panted, moving in rhythm with Margot's fingers.

Margot chuckled, the sound low and incredibly sexy. "That's *my* good girl."

Jack's focus slipped as she was consumed by pleasure, Margot murmuring dirty little nothings into her ear as she continued to work her clit. Her nerves held her on a razors edge as she clung to Margot, tilted her head back and felt Margot's breath against her throat.

"M-Merr-Margot," she stammered, bringing the woman's face up to hers and kissing her deeply. "I'm —"

Her orgasm thrummed through her before she could get the words out.

Jack started to laugh as she came, hard, all over the beautiful bookstore owner's fingers, the idea and euphoria of it almost too much to bear.

Margot lifted her fingers up to inspect, which Jack quickly took hold of and stuck them in her mouth, sucking her own juices off of Margot's pretty fingers.

Margot pouted. "You didn't even let me taste you."

Jack kissed her messily, drawing her tongue over Margot's in a soft game of chase, before she slid her leg between Margot's thighs, pulling the woman's ass up closer to her.

"You think we're done, Merry? How else are we supposed to stay warm in a bookstore without any heat?"

Jack was pretty sure that the sound of Margot's delighted laughter was all that she needed to hear for the rest of her life.

Much later, they were tangled a mess of limbs and blankets. Margot's head rested against Jack's shoulder, one of her perfect legs draped over Jack's stomach.

Jack trailed her fingers repeatedly over Margot's scalp, messing the curls there, marvelling at their feel beneath her hand. Wasn't it just today, mere moments ago, when she had wondered what it would feel like to run her hands through them?

Some Christmas dreams do come true, she thought, a stupid, drunk with happiness smile stretching across her face.

"What?" said Margot dreamily.

"I'm just thinking how quiet it is in here," said Jack. The sound of the storm outside had picked up again, the soft tinkling of snowflakes against the glass an orchestra to their night.

"Mmm." Margot nodded into Jack's skin, nuzzling in closer.

"I think we should put on more of those silly tunes."

"Silly?"

"The oldies. The good ones, as you said."

Margot pushed up on one elbow to look down at Jack. Her hair tumbled around her face, lit by the colourful hue of the Christmas lights around them.

Jack trailed a finger along Margot's cheek. "You are so beautiful, you know that?"

Margot's eyes melted as she bent down to kiss Jack, carefully, delicately, tasting of sex and Christmas, before she pushed herself up to go track down her Bluetooth speaker.

Jack watched Margot pad across the store, hurrying back as the woman tucked her arms around her.

"It's chilly as tits in here," she complained, immediately tucking herself back into place at Jack's side and wrapping them in a blanket, before she hooked up her phone. "I only have a little battery life left, but it should last us for a little music. Billie Holiday or Frank Sinatra?"

"Anything you want."

Jack kissed the side of Margot's head as she started to thumb through the playlist.

The moment that Mariah Carey came blasting through the speakers, Jack knew for sure that she was a goner for this woman. Maybe it was the Christmas magic that she thought she'd lost long ago, coming back one last time to give her the best Christmas she'd ever had.

Jack started to sing along to the incredibly overplayed, frankly overly commercialized song, letting her voice crack and pitch up as much as it would go. Margot howled as she turned up the volume, the two of them singing at the top of their lungs.

She was never going to let this woman go, Jack realized later as Margot and her were curled up together, both of them back in some semblance of clothing — just the comfortable bits, there was no way in any life she was putting on her cold jeans now — as the temperature of the shop dipped a little lower. Margot's speaker played Christmas music softly, a mix of the oldies and the modern-day songs.

"Read me something," said Jack, feeling perfectly, wonderfully sleepy, even though she didn't want this moment to end. She wanted to somehow bottle this feeling, this exact moment, and keep it locked inside a snow globe for as long as she was alive.

"Alright."

Margot shifted out of their cozy corner once more before returning with the beautiful edition of Jane Austen's *Emma* she'd been holding earlier, pressed to her chest like a talisman against the horror of the leak.

"I used to read this every Christmas with my grandma," said Margot softly. "It was her favourite book. She would read it to me all the time, telling me one day I would find my Knightley and we would live happily ever after."

"Too bad you found me, then."

"I don't know, you fit the mold pretty well," said Margot, flipping through the pages, searching for something. "Slightly grumpy, not overly talkative unless you somehow get trapped in a bookstore on Christmas Eve eve and drink copious amounts of hot chocolate."

"I am just the right amount of talkative."

Margot looked at her with a soft smile and kissed her. "You are for me, Mr. Knightley."

She settled back against Jack again, the two of them snuggling in close.

"This is the Christmas scene," explained Margot.

"Read on, Miss Woodhouse."

Jack closed her eyes and leaned her cheek on Margot's head as she started to read. The Christmas song in the background started to sing about chestnuts and fires, the sound swirling around the two of them, blanketing Jack's mood in a perfect sense of comfort. She listened to the cadence of Margot's voice, her tone perfectly suited for the rise and fall of reading a book.

"'Christmas weather,' observed Mr. Elton. 'Quite seasonable; and extremely fortunate we may think ourselves that it did not begin yesterday, and prevent this day's party, which it might very possibly have done,'..."

9

Merry and Bright

Margot Merry

Margot blinked awake wearily as thin, bright morning light leaked in through the window above her. For a moment, she couldn't quite remember where she was. She breathed out long and slow, gently stretching like a cat who had just awoken in a sunbeam. It was warm and soft all around her, despite her back complaining at the fact she was on the floor.

The floor.

Then came the familiar sound of scraping, muted and dull. Margot sat up, casting a glance around her at the piles of blankets and books and weird things they had brought into their little corner of the bookshop over the evening. Her jeans and parka still sat in a heap a little way off, and she cringed, knowing she was going to have to put those back on at some point.

Then she remembered why they had come off, and exactly how they had come off, the night before. A soft warmth ran through her. It really happened, didn't it? The blackout, the leak, the kiss...

"Jack?"

There was no response, other than the soft scraping outside.

Margot stood, taking a blanket with her and draping it over her shoulders like a cape. She padded toward the front, following the sound.

The storm had stopped sometime during the night, leaving an absolutely massive amount of snow behind. Some of the front windows were nearly fully covered by the banks and drifts, light peeking through at the top. The power, too, had come back on; the lights she hadn't turned off the day before all back on. A soft whirring came to her ears then, from somewhere in her shop.

Margot ducked into the empty collections room, staring at the series of fans that were now plugged in and whirring at top speed.

Jack.

At that thought, she walked to the front again and pulled open the door to the shop, revealing a winter wonderland. The drifts had entirely erased any sign of her and Jack's nighttime fun outside, except for the very top of Frosty's head, which was just visible from his eyes up, staring at her.

And of course, in the middle of the pathway, struggling mightily to clear the snow with nothing more than Margot's inadequate tiny shovel, was Jaqueline Bright, bundled in her parka and knobbly rainbow toque. Margot leaned against the doorway and smiled, her heart aching softly as she watched the woman shovel. The soft look of concentration on Jack's face as she reached up, trying to chip at the large bank of snow in front of the shop, practically melted Margot's entire soul.

The shift that erupted over Jack's face as she noticed Margot standing there, wrapped up in a blanket watching her, that was what settled Margot in her certainty. God, she liked this woman.

"Happy Christmas Eve," she said quietly, her voice buffeting out in a cloud of air.

"Happy Christmas Eve to you, Merry."

Jack pushed the shovel in the nearby bank and left it there, her attention fully on Margot as she walked over, already taking off her mitts. Without hesitating, Jack held both sides of Margot's jaw and pulled her in for the most sweet, perfect kiss. It left Margot slightly breathless, dizzy, and filled to the brim with bubbles.

"Well good morning to you too," she said, having to hold onto the front of Jack's parka to stay standing.

"What say you to a cinnamon bun for breakfast? I can even heat it up a little on your grandma's camp stove."

"That sounds perfect."

The two of them slipped inside, Jack sliding off her winter boots and throwing down her parka. As they both settled back into their cozy corner together, Jack readying the pastries for breakfast, Margot curled up against her side. They didn't really need to say anything more, as they waited for the buns to heat through; it was the perfect silence, companionable, together.

Whatever was to come — in the next few minutes as they ate, or in the next couple of hours as they finally made their way home through the snow, or in the next few days as holiday celebrations continued, Margot knew that she wanted to be with Jack.

Whatever they had started, here amidst the stacks, beneath the battery powered Christmas lights together, it was good. *Really* good.

Because of course it was. How could it not be when you have both Merry and Bright in one place at Christmas?

Acknowledgements

They say that writing is an incredibly solitary activity — and while it is, the community you build is next to nothing I've come across in my life yet.

This project all started when I decided, on a whim, to write a novella in a couple of months to try and submit to a holiday romance contest. I reached out to a few friends to help me brainstorm, and suddenly, Jack and Margot were leaping out of my brain, almost fully formed. It was a challenge for me, as a novel writer (and a self-proclaimed over writer) to dive into such a short project, AND one that was straight up contemporary romance, but I was excited for the journey.

Thank you first to Sofia, Sophie, and Yelani for being the first to help me brainstorm my way through the preliminary thoughts and vibes of the story; without you there to encourage me to try this out, this novella would never have existed. Sofia, without you and your penchant for romance books and the spicier elements in those pages, I'm pretty sure that I would never have even thought to include the content in chapter 7 and 8. To both you and Sophie for championing more spice, I thank you!! And for you three, Sofia, Sophie, and Yelani, being constant consumers and purveyors of romance novels, sharing what you loved and what you hated; every single bit of it has helped in me crafting this story.

Thank you also to Ally, my lovely online friend who graciously beta read this novella and gave me her thoughts in an incredibly quick turn around. I too think this book rates about an eight out of nine reindeers on a Christmassy scale! And thank you too, Ally, for being an incredible champion for this work, and all my other works and ideas, and whatever else we share on a daily basis. I appreciate you so, so much.

And thank you to Julie and Laura, two of my ARC readers, who were able to catch some typos for me. Typos, as you all kknow, will Hhaunt me forvever!

Thank you again, specially, to Yelani, who agreed to be my editor for this project. Yelani, you absolutely knocked it out of the park in helping me take this story and elevate it, working with me to ensure that it could be the best it could be. Just so you know, you won't ever be able to get rid of me as a client, because now that I've tasted this greatness, I don't ever want to stop.

And finally, thank you to all my lovely friends in my online community I've curated over on YouTube, TikTok, and Instagram. You're always hyping me and my projects up, showing up with excitement and genuine happiness whenever I accomplish something and have new, crazy ideas to share.

We'll see what else I've got up my sleeve!

About the Author

Jenn Collignon is a Canadian author and content creator based out of the prairies, who loves everything fantasy. This is her first foray into romance, but you can find her other cozy and fantastical books under the pseudonym J. A. Collignon. Jenn is an avid member of the bookish internet community through her Youtube channel, Tiktok, Instagram, and Twitter. Follow her to keep up to date on future book releases.

Youtube: Jenn's Bookshelf
Tiktok: @jennsbookshelf
Instagram: @authorjacollignon
Twitter: @BookshelfJenn